BEING A FRIEND

BLACK
RABBIT
BOOKS

PEGGY
SNOW

Ways to Make Friends

It's fun to have friends. But first, you have to make friends. Introduce yourself with, "Hi, I'm (say your name). What's your name?" Smile and look the person in the eye.

If someone acts friendly toward you, act friendly back. Try asking questions like, "What's your favorite kind of music?" Or say something nice like, "Cool shoes!"

Did You Know?
To be a friend to others, it helps to like yourself. When you like yourself, it shows. People want to be around you.

Be a Good Listener

2

Did You Know?
Listening takes **patience**. Wait until your friend is done talking. Share something about yourself when it's your turn.

Friends have conversations with each other. They take turns talking. They listen when the other person is talking.

What are ways to show you're listening? Look your friend in the eye. Say, "All right!" or "Yeah!" or "That's cool!"

Nod your head to show you understand or agree. Ask questions to show you're paying attention. Try not to interrupt or get distracted.

Be Helpful

Friends help each other. That's what friends do. Helping shows you care about someone.

What are ways to help a friend? You can pick up toys after a playdate. You can do homework together. You can push your friend's swing on the playground.

Kind words are helpful too. When a friend is **struggling**, say, "You can do it!" When a friend succeeds, say, "That was awesome!"

Think About It
What are more ways
to help a friend?

Be
Kind

Friends are kind to each other. Kindness is good for everyone. When you're kind to others, they feel happy. You feel happy too.

What are ways to be kind? You can ask someone, "Do you want to play?" You can share your toys and snacks. You can ask your friend, "What do YOU want to do?"

Be your kindest when a friend is feeling down. Spend time with your friend. Give them a hug.

Did You Know?

Treat others like you want to be treated. That's the Golden Rule.

Stand Up for
Your Friends

Friends have each other's backs. They watch out for each other. They stand up for each other.

If you see a friend being bullied, what can you do? Act strong and confident. Say, "Stop!" or "That's not cool!" Stay calm and hold your head high. With your friend, get away from the bully. Then tell an adult. Adults need to know when bad things happen to kids so they can help.

Think About It

Name an adult you
trust and can talk to.

Where to Find
Friends

19

You don't need a million friends. It's OK to have one or two good friends. But what if you want to make new friends? Think about things you're interested in. Baseball? Dancing? Singing? Chess? Find people who have things in common with you.

Look for a club, group, class, or team. Visit a community center to see what's up. Ask a parent or teacher for help and ideas.

Did You Know?

Someone wants to be your friend.

FANTASTIC FACTS

Having friends boosts your self-esteem.

Friendship is good for your health.

Having friends can help you cope with hard times.

Having friends gives you a sense of belonging. That's something humans need.

Spending time with good friends reduces stress.

Babies understand friendship before they can walk or talk.

COOL COMPARISONS

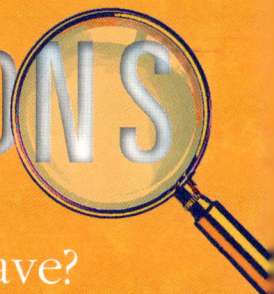

How many close friends do people have?

Two to three
30%

One
7%

Six to nine
12%

None
12%

Three to four
24%

Ten or more
13%

23

MORE TO EXPLORE
RESOURCES

Glossary

confident (KAHN-fuh-dent) Feeling sure about yourself and your actions.

conversation (kahn-vur-SAY-shuhn) Talking with someone and exchanging thoughts.

distracted (dis-TRAK-tuhd) Unable to focus.

interrupt (in-tuh-RUHPT) To start talking when someone else is speaking. To make another person stop talking.

patience (PAY-shenss) The ability to wait in a calm manner.

struggling (STRUG-ling) Trying very hard to do something.

Read More

Crohn, JoAnn. *Me and My Friendships.* New York: Rockridge Press, 2021.

Schuh, Mari C. *Patience.* Minneapolis: Jump!, Inc., 2021.

Index

TOP RANK is published by Black Rabbit Books, P.O. Box 227, Mankato, MN, 56002. • COPYRIGHT © 2025 Black Rabbit Books. All rights reserved. No part of this book may be reproduced in any form without written permission from the publisher. • Top Rank is an imprint of Black Rabbit Books • Edited by Alissa Thielges • Designed by Danny Nanos • Photographs © Getty: 10'000 Hours, 8–9, Aptyp_koK, 20, ArtMarie, 2, 15, Cultura RM Exclusive/Sporrer/Rupp, 13, Image Source, cover, 16–17,Klaus Vedfelt, 17, Reggie Casagrande, 6–7, SolStock, 10–11, Thomas Barwick, 21; Shutterstock: Cheryl Casey, 14, Jacek Chabraszewski, 19, Jacob Lund, 18, LightField Studios, 4, Ljupco Smokovski, 11, Lunaraa, 23, Prostock-studio, cover, Roman Samborskyi, 5, Vectorfusionart, 12 • Printed in the United States of America

Library of Congress Cataloging-in-Publication Data: Names: Snow, Peggy, author. | Title: Being a friend / by Peggy Snow. | Description: Mankato, MN: Black Rabbit Books, 2025. | Series: Top rank: healthy and happy | Includes bibliographical references and index. | Ages 8–11 | Grades 4–6 | Identifiers: LCCN 2023058220 | ISBN 9781632357946 (library binding) | ISBN 9781645820727 (ebook) | Subjects: LCSH: Friendship—Juvenile literature. | Classification: LCC BF575.F66 S62595 2025 | DDC 177/.62—dc23/eng/20240130 | LC record available at https://lccn.loc.gov/2023058220